I0537742

Copyright © Marta Moran Bishop

May 22, 2023

ISBN: 978-1-939484-58-1

https://martamoranbishop.com

Cover by Stephen Walker

https://srwalkerdesigns.com

THE MICE OF BARNVILLE

EPISODE ONE — THE QUEST

By

Marta Moran Bishop

In the beginning, these short stories were inspired by the ongoing fight I had to keep the mice from digging under the horses' mats. And into the barn to get the bits of hay and grain our horses left behind.

No matter what I used to fill in the 2-to-5-inch holes that these tiny rascals insisted on digging, nothing worked to keep them from burrowing along the wall under the mats inside stalls next to the wall of the tack room. They'd move it. The peppermint balls that are supposed to be deterrents didn't work. They just moved them. I wondered what they did with the manure, sand, and peppermint balls. They were moving it out and obviously putting it somewhere. But how and why?

Afterward, my husband and I joked about what the mice might be doing with the manure and peppermint balls. I wanted to give my friend Stephen Walker a chuckle and told him the story. As Stephen is the best graphic artist in the business, with a great sense of humor, he began sending me mice graphics that inspired me to write these short stories that are becoming episodes of what is going on under our barn.

I dedicate this book to the two of them—Ken and Stephen, each of whom are both supportive and have inspired me to pursue this series of short tails. Oops! Episodic tales.

THE JOURNEY

Scampering across the field, pants hanging nearly around his ankles, Joshua yelled. "Uncle Horace, Uncle Horace, I found it!"

"I'm over here, Joshua. Now pull up your pants. They are falling down again. You, being such a skinny young mouse, should wear suspenders or at least a string to keep them up? Now, what did you find?"

Looking through the spectacles that covered the rheumy eyes of his great-great uncle, he replied. "This is the perfect place for our new home, and I found it!"

"Here's a bit of string." He said, pulling it out of his pocket and tying it around the waist of the young mouse. "If we are to be scampering around, you'll need it." He felt proud of still being able to see as well as he did in the bright sunlight after spending so many years underground in the dark. Horace tugged at his white eyebrows, pushed his glasses up, and tightly gripped his walking stick, as he stated. "Lead on. Let's go see what you found, Joshua, and if it is as you say, you'll get special honor in our kingdom. But please slow down. I don't move as fast as I once did."

"Okay, Uncle Horace, follow me."

Through the jungle of brush and tall trees, Joshua led the way. Followed by Uncle Horace hobbling along, holding tight to his cane. About twenty others, who couldn't resist seeing what Joshua had found, followed behind. Murmurs went through the group.

"Do you think it is possible that such a young one found a new home for us, Homer?" Merle asked his tall, handsome cousin.

Looking at his roly-poly cousin, Homer declared. "Joshua has always been one to seek adventure, never listening to his elders about being careful and such. It is possible, Merle." he said, his eyes full of hope and doubt. "But we must follow every path open to us."

"Hurry, you all. We've been homeless for a while now and your Aunt Tabby is nearly due to pup, and we have nowhere safe for her to have her babies. It's not safe out in the open with just a few leaves to cover her from the prying eyes of those who would be all too happy to have her and her pups for dinner." Jethro added.

Following closely behind his larger cousin, he uttered. "It'll be lucky for us if Joshua really found us a new home."

"We know you are anxious about your mate and soon to come pups. We all feel the same and if it was our mate, we'd be in a panic, too, Jethro." "If so, a new home," began Merle, "then I hope it'll be large enough for the entire clan, and Homer."

"I agree, Merle."

"It's horrible that we had to abandon our old home. Why did that huge, two-legged creature feel a need to throw Aunt Maisie's pups out of the shed? They were so small and needed a warm, dry place," Merle said, his whiskers atwitter.

Judah scurried along behind, frowning, perpetually asking why, why, why."

"I don't know," began the wise Homer, "but when they did that and sealed up all our food sources, we had to leave. It was just too dangerous for us to live there by then."

Judah persisted with another why.

Homer patiently replied, "If we had to go out to forage for food, fighting off Eagles, Hawks, Rats, Squirrels, cats, and the occasional snake. But the humans, they are the most dangerous of all."

"Besides," added Merle, "there wasn't enough room for all of us."

Judah asked the elder, "Do you think Maisie will ever have pups again, or is she too sad to try? I mean, it's possible, that is, if she feels safe enough, but only then might she get over her grief."

"I'm hoping she does, Judah. "It's possible that if she feels safe enough, she might get over her heartache. She'd be so much happier with little ones around." Homer replied sadly, as he helped his older cousin up the cliff of rocks.

"Do you really think she will, Homer?"

"I'm sure she will, Judah."

"Come on, you two, we must make sure we keep up with Joshua. He scampers so quickly. Lucky for us that Great-great Uncle Horace is slower." Merle stated as they all scrambled over the rocks and through the jungle, all of them keeping their eyes open for predators. Jethro's eyes constantly moving, peering into every leaf and under each rock.

"Here, let me give you a hand up Jethro, I don't mean to be rude, but you are getting a bit round about the middle and Aunt Tabby will need you for a long time. Not that you aren't still the handsome fellow. What are you looking for anyway, Jethro?"

"I try to keep my weight down, but Tabby lays out such a fine table, Homer. Thanks for the help on the rocks." He exclaimed to his handsome cousin, wiping the sweat from his brow. "I'm making sure there aren't any predators around here. After all, so many things can lurk among the rocks and in this jungle. Homer, I wonder how young Joshua found this place. Did he say?"

"He didn't it is a mystery. What with this being such a jungle and the rocks are so steep. It's amazing that he ever looked back here. I'll give you a hand over this bit. It seems as if we are through the worst of the rocks now, Jethro."

"Homer, it's so hot today. Can you still see Uncle Horace? We haven't gotten lost, have we?"

"I can still see him, Jethro. But just barely. We'll have to hurry a bit more, and you are right, it is boiling today, Jethro." Homer said as he pulled Jethro over the last rock and wiped the sweat off his whiskers.

"Hurry up, everyone," Merle called back at them.

"Thank the Mouse King. I think we are all over the rock cliff now. Do you see that huge wooden building in front of us?" Silas yelled back.

"We see it, Silas, but some of us aren't as fit as you are, and we take a while longer to get up the rock cliff. I hope there is an easier way to get into our new home from the south."

"Your Aunt Tabby and the little ones will never make it up this cliff," Raul cried as he looked back at his cousins as they struggled up the cliff. He watched despairingly as Cousin Homer pushed his middle-aged, plump, and lazy brother, Ryker, up the last of the huge rocks that lined the cliff. *It's a good thing Homer is so big and fit. He thought.*

"Will someone help Chester? You'll know he has that bad foot from catching it in a mousetrap." Raul yelled back.

"I'll help him after I help Ryker." Homer said with a frown.

"Is anyone watching out for mousetraps or snakes?" Chester whined loudly.

"Chester, why did you come with us? You are such a fraidy-cat, I'd have thought you'd stay back at the camp with the others." Homer asked.

"It's my job to protect everyone, Homer. No one watches out for you all carefully enough. Not to mention Joshua just goes his merry way without a thought for all that can happen. Thanks for the hand up. These rocks are really difficult to maneuver."

"No problem, Chester." Homer said with a sigh. But finally, every mouse stood atop a grassy knoll and stared at their would-be new home, a huge, well-kept, warm-looking home in the near distance. Joshua had indeed found something looking special.

THE JOURNEY'S OVER

Finally, the last of the troupe reached the top. There was a path along the back of the barn and they could easily see Uncle Horace holding back those that had reached him first. His whiskers twitched. He wiped the sweat from his brow with one hand, the other resting heavily on his cane. After wiping his brow, he lifted his hand in the air.

"There is an entrance that goes under this structure, but we do not know if anyone lives in there yet. Caution must be used."

"Uncle Horace, how are we to know if we don't go in?" asked Chester, still panting from the climb.

"This will require smart calculation. We must have a plan."

"What do you suggest?' Raul called from the back of the group.

"Please come up closer, Raul. You are one of the most fit in the group, and one of our best warriors, too."

Raul swaggered through the crowded group. Not used to being singled out, he held his head higher today.

"Do you have any suggestions, Raul?"

"Uncle Horace, we should see who brought their spears with them. If they don't have them, we need to make some. I don't believe we should go exploring in the dark either, not without being able to see into every corner."

"Exactly right. Alright, we need those who have their spears with them to come to the front. Those who can whittle them stay at the back and please work quickly. We don't want to leave the littlest or the women who are with pups alone too long without enough protection."

The plumpest of the group wiggled their way to the back, bumping into those going to the front. "Hey, watch out, Ryker, you almost knocked me off the cliff."

"Sorry, Homer." Ryker said as he began picking up branches that were strewn across the path at the back of the barn. He sat on the ground, with those chosen to whittle, and began to make spears in his own lazy fashion.

"Who among you is experienced in making some form of light that won't burn anything down?" Uncle Horace asked.

"Why do we need light, Uncle Horace?"

"That's a good question, Sebastian," He replied to the slightly puggy young man. "I know you are one of our best warriors and see very well in the dark, but all of us don't and we might miss something dangerous lurking in a crevice or corner."
"Like a snake," added Joshua.

"Uncle Horace, I think I can scavenge something to hold a flame safely. But we will need more than one if we are to make sure every inch is safe in there." Gasper stated. "Ignoring Sebastian's question.

"You have always been a very good builder, Gasper, thank you. Please pick out those that can help you the most. No one, and I mean no one, goes near that doorway until we are ready," Horace's cousin Redd shouted."

"Raul, please gather all your fellow warriors and stand guard. No one is to go into the entrance until we are ready. I'll be right back. Your Uncle Redd and I need to have a brief conference."

The crowd in the area parted for Horace and Redd, moving as one toward the rear. Still, Redd noisily and unnecessarily ordered the younger mice to move.

"You don't need to shout or get bossy, Redd. I know how hard it is to be the younger brother. Once I was one, and someday you will need to become the leader here." Horace cautioned his younger brother quietly.

"You are still young, Horace."

"Not that young, Redd. I'm feeling my age these days. Don't worry so much about filling my shoes. You'll find your own way if you let yourself."

"Horace, you always tell everyone what to do. Why is it different with me?"

"It's in the tone of your voice, Redd. That's all. You sound gruff."
"I'll work on that, Horace. But I don't enjoy thinking about you being gone."

"None of us lives forever, Redd. Now I need to go back up to the front. Please help me keep things going here."

"Thanks Horace,. I'll have your back."

THE ENTRANCE

Moving back to the entrance under the barn, Horace stated. "We need a few of you to remain on lookout when we go in."

"What will we be looking for, Uncle Horace?"

"Anything that might attack us, either outside of our possible new home, or if something escapes from the inside when we are looking around. I hope that answers your question, Joshua? I believe that you and Judah would be quite suited to that job."

"Why me? I want to go in too. I found the entrance."

"Yes, you did, and we are all thankful for it. But you are too young and not trained as a warrior. There will be other important tasks for you soon. Don't worry, when the time comes, you will get your chance to see what is in there." Horace answered, pushing his spectacles back up on his nose.

"I've got it," Gasper said, holding up a small hollowed-out stone with a small flame lit in it. Behind him stood five mice holding their own little hollowed-out stones. Each held a small flame.

"Wonderful Gasper. Now we are about ready. Homer, Raul, Jethro, Otis, Gus, Lincoln, Lamorat, Lester, take an extra spear with you, from the stack that Ryker and his buddies made. We are going in.
Every mouse's whiskers stood up. "Gasper: you and your group, please stay behind the warriors, but make sure you follow as close as possible without getting in their way."

"Where will you be, Uncle Horace?" Gasper asked.

"I'll be going in with our warriors."

"Not first?"

"Yes, I'll be first in, but with our warriors right beside me. Redd, I'd like you with me. You are keen-eyed."

"I'm coming, Horace. Tucker, please keep everyone else out until we come tell you it's safe, please. We'll still need a guard out here to make sure nothing comes up behind us. Would you assign someone to that?" He said to his good-looking, strong son.

"Yes, sir," Tucker said as he took his spear and moved up near the group that would go into the door.

"Look at the size of that doorway. Something big might be in there! You can't both go in at the same time, Uncle Horace? What if there are feral cats, rats, snakes, or maybe the farmer put mousetraps in there? We can't take the chance of losing you." Chester moaned in his high-pitched, nasally voice.

"It's our job, Chester, and we must have a new home. Now stand back, please. Get behind the others. That limp of yours might give us all away!"

Chester blanched at the mention of his stiff leg, and he gravely said, "Yes, sir, I'll guard our rear in case something evil comes up behind us!"

"Stay with those that can protect you. But move back, Chester." Uncle Horace replied, oblivious to having hurt Chester's feelings as the elder only twirled his whiskers. Fully concentrating instead on his plan of attack, he suddenly shouted to Chester.

"Come back here and stand with us, Chester. We'll protect you and Joshua," Abe declared. And with Tucker's help, they ushered him them to the back.

A NEW HOME?

"I believe we are all ready now, or at least as ready as we can be. Raul, Homer, and Gasper, you come in with me. Jethro, Otis and Farren, please come in with your Uncle Redd. The rest of you enter slowly, and all of you keep your spears or lanterns at ready."

"Oh, dear!" Shouted Chester. "They are going in that doorway. What if something is in there?"

"It's big enough for an elephant to pass through," added Otis.

"I've heard elephants fear us," Merle said bravely.

Hearing this, the entire group began a loud, growing twittering.

"Silence! Please," Redd firmly shut this noise down. With everyone screwing up their courage, they started under the enormous hole that went

under the barn and was the door to what might
be their new home.

Raul, Homer, and Uncle Horace, followed closely
by Gasper, entered as the forward explorers. Their
small, bead-sized eyes worked quite well in the
dimness below ground where they had bored
canals for their safety. "It has a nice wood ceiling
above us. Do you see it, Redd?"

"I do, Horace. It will do well to keep the weather
out. The space is large, but I believe we can
hollow out more of it. That would enable the
entire clan to live here, and there would still be
room for the children and grandchildren to
come."

"Raul, Homer, and the rest of you, please check
every nook and cranny. Something...anything
might...well really must've lived here at one time,
if not now! Still, with luck, whatever it was...or is
may've smelled us coming and perhaps they or it
has left."

"We are on it, Uncle Horace. Should we leave anyone behind with you and Uncle Redd?"

"I think only two of you need to stay with us, just encase mind you. What do you think, Redd?"

"I agree with you, Horace. The place has a vacant air about it. I don't believe anything or anyone has been living here for a long time."

"I agree with you, Redd, but you all go check things out anyway. Keep your spears up. We don't wish anyone hurt or to be surprised." Horace stated as the two brothers began exploring.

"Gasper, can you come over here, please?"

Holding his small light in one hand and scampering over on three paws, Gasper hurried over. "What can I do for you, Uncle Redd?"

"Does that look as if it was once a front door?"

Setting his light down on the dirt and eyed the area closely before answering. Gasper said. "Uncle Redd, you are right. It appears that it was a front door. I don't think it would take much to open it up again. Someone did a poor job of closing it. Though I see bits of mice poison in the sand. So, we will need to be careful. I believe a few sticks tied together will remove the poison and clear the opening at the same time."

"That is excellent. While you are all making sure there is nothing left in here, I'm going to go out and send Joshua and his cousin Bertram around the side of the barn. Just to make sure no one is in front before we begin opening up the doorway."

"Horace, are you okay with me leaving for a bit?"

"Absolutely Redd. Your idea is great. I'll just have a little more of a look around while you are gone. I might even take a brief rest and write some notes, while Gasper is getting his tools together. Why

don't you send Merle in to help Gasper while you
are out there?"

"The others are going to want to come in,
Horace."

"Of course they will. Please have your son Tucker
make them wait a bit more. We want to make
sure it's safe, and I'd like to know about the front
door first."

"What should I tell them, Horace?"

"Use your discretion, Redd, I trust you. I don't
believe they will have long to wait, though."

"Nor do I. We don't want Chester in here until we
can prove it is really safe," Redd said as he
scampered through the darkness. *Barnville, that
will be the name of our new home.* He thought as
he went out the doorway into the daylight.

Meanwhile, Horace sat quietly scribbling notes about what they'd need to make this unique place a home.

Dear Reader: This is not The End but only Episode One. Further Episodes of *The Mice of Barnville* will continue the story...